Riley Rye, Private Eye

Level 9 – Gold

Helpful Hints for Reading at Home

The focus phonemes (units of sound) used throughout this series are in line with the order in which your child is taught at school. This offers a consistent approach to learning whether reading at home or in the classroom.

HERE ARE SOME COMMON WORDS THAT YOUR CHILD MIGHT FIND TRICKY:

water	where	would	know	thought	through	couldn't
laughed	eyes	once	we're	school	can't	our

TOP TIPS FOR HELPING YOUR CHILD TO READ:

- Encourage your child to read aloud as well as silently to themselves.
- Allow your child time to absorb the text and make comments.
- Ask simple questions about the text to assess understanding.
- Encourage your child to clarify the meaning of new vocabulary.

This book focuses on developing independence, fluency and comprehension. It is a gold level 9 book band.

Nanny gave a little snore from her chair in the corner. Ant sighed. Nanny was no fun at all. She always made Ant go to bed super early.

Ant thought Nanny might just be the most boring person in the whole world.

THE NINJA

"Up next, we have more news on the Ninja," said the reporter on the TV. "He was spotted again last night helping an old lady across the road. Police still have no idea who the Ninja might be."

Ant sat up and listened closely. Stories about the Ninja were the only parts of the news he was interested in.

The Ninja was the city's mysterious new superhero. He dressed head to toe in black, with a red bandana tied around his head. He jumped through the shadows and across roofs, helping people in trouble and catching criminals.

Then the Ninja tied up the bad guys with one of his bandanas and left them outside the police station.

Ant thought he was awesome. Ant looked out of the window, hoping to spot the Ninja jumping past.

"Bedtime, Ant," said Nanny. Ant jumped. When had she woken up?

"But it's still early!" said Ant. "I want to look out for the Ninja."

"Not more Ninja nonsense," Nanny muttered. "You must be tired. I know I am. Off you go."

Nanny let out a loud yawn and shooed Ant off to his room.

Ant couldn't believe it. How could Nanny be tired? She had only just woken up! And how could she possibly call the Ninja nonsense?

Chapter 2

Ant lay in bed thinking about the Ninja. He imagined what it would be like jumping from roof to roof, chasing down bad guys.

Then Ant heard a crash in the kitchen. What if it was a burglar? Maybe the Ninja would come! Ant had to go and see.

He crept down the hall. More noises came from the dark kitchen. Someone was in there.

Ant switched on the kitchen light and couldn't believe his eyes. There, dressed from head to toe in black, tying a red bandana around her head, was Nanny.

"But... you can't be the Ninja!" Ant said.

"Why ever not?" asked Nanny.

Ant thought for a moment.

"Because you're old!" he finally said.

Nanny chuckled and went over to the open window.

"Wait!" said Ant. "What if you get hurt?"

"I can look after myself," Nanny said.

"Wait!" Ant said again. "Can I come with you? You can't leave me alone. You're supposed to be looking after me."

Ant was sure Nanny was going to say no. Nanny never let him do anything fun.

But then her eyes twinkled.

"Come on!" she said with a grin.

Chapter 3

Ant hung on to Nanny's back like a rucksack as Nanny climbed up the drainpipe. Ant never knew Nanny was so strong. Ant tried not to look down as Nanny climbed higher and higher. Finally they made it to the roof.

Ant could see the whole city from up there.

"Hold tight," said Nanny. "I hope you're ready."

"Ready for what?" Ant asked.

Nanny ran towards the edge of the roof.
She wasn't... she couldn't possibly... she was.
Nanny was going to jump off the roof!

"Stop!" said Ant.

But Nanny didn't stop. Ant shut his eyes and waited for them to crash to the ground. But they didn't. They were soaring through the air. Nanny landed on the next roof, ran across it, and then leapt again. Ant felt like he was flying.

"How are you doing this?" Ant asked.

"A ninja never reveals her secrets," Nanny said with a smile.

Then Ant heard a noise. Was someone in danger? Maybe Ant had ninja senses like Nanny.

"I think someone is in trouble," said Ant.

"I'll go and investigate," Nanny said. From somewhere in her tight Ninja outfit, Nanny pulled out a long wire with a hook on the end. She threw it, and it hooked somewhere on the ground. Nanny tied the other end to the roof.

"Stay here," Nanny told Ant.

"But…" Ant didn't want to miss out. But Nanny had already clipped herself to the rope. She flew down it like a zip wire. Then she disappeared into the shadows.

The zip wire looked so cool, Ant couldn't resist having a go himself. He was sure Nanny wouldn't mind.

He threw his jumper over the rope and held tightly to the sleeves.

Then he jumped.

Chapter 4

WHOOOOOSH!

Ant whizzed down the wire.

This was fun! Then Ant heard a

RRRRIIIIIPPP!

His jumper was splitting.

"Oh no!" Ant cried as he fell.

He landed with a **CRASH!** in a huge stinky rubbish bin.

Nanny stared down at him. She didn't look happy.

"Sorry, Nanny," Ant said. "I thought you might need rescuing."

"From a kitten?" Nanny chuckled, as a tiny fluffy fur ball jumped onto Ant's head.

Ant felt embarrassed. Maybe he didn't have ninja senses after all.

"I wish I could be a ninja like you," Ant said. Nanny looked at Ant's sad face.

"I can teach you," said Nanny. "But it isn't easy. Follow me."

Nanny climbed up the drainpipe. She made it look simple. Ant tried to follow. The pipe was slippery. His hands wouldn't grip. Nanny had made it to the top already. Ant felt useless.

"Ninjas never give up," Nanny said. "Keep trying."

Ant tried again. And again. Slowly, he made it up to the roof.

"I did it!" he said.

"Very good," Nanny said. "Next, we jump."

"I can't!" said Ant.

He looked at the gap between the rooftops. It wasn't that far. But the ground looked a very long way down. What if he didn't make it? Ant's knees turned to jelly.

"Watch me," Nanny said. She took a run up and jumped.

It was like her legs were made of springs. She flew through the air and landed safely on the other side.

Ant took a deep breath. He had to do it if he ever wanted to be a Ninja. He took a run up.

And then he did the biggest jump he could.

Time seemed to slow down as Ant flew through the air.

Finally he landed with a bump on the other side. He had made it! Nanny grinned at him.

"Not bad," she said. "Come on, then, let's go."

Chapter 5

Ant and Nanny jumped from roof to roof. Ant felt on top of the world. He wasn't as quick as Nanny, but he was getting better.

Then they heard a loud crash. An alarm started screeching. This time Ant knew something was wrong. They peered down over the edge of the roof. It was a bank robbery!

"Stay here," Nanny said.

This time, Ant listened. He was enjoying his Ninja training, but he definitely wasn't ready to fight off bad guys yet.

Nanny jumped across to a lamppost and slid down it. Ant watched as she crept into the bank.

Then he waited... and waited. He was getting worried.

Then a robber came out of the bank. He was getting away. But where was Nanny? What if she was in trouble?

Ant had to do something. And quickly.

This time Ant didn't hesitate. He had to save Nanny and stop the robber from getting away.

Ant jumped. His hands grabbed the lamp post. He whizzed down it and landed with a bump on something hard and lumpy. He had landed right on top of the bank robber!

"Got you!" cried Ant.

Nanny came out of the bank, dragging the other two robbers with her. She looked at Ant in surprise.

"Well," she said, "maybe you'll make a good ninja after all!"

Nanny threw Ant one of her bandanas. He quickly tied up the robber.

The sun was starting to rise as they left the bank robbers outside the police station.

"Not bad for a night's work," Nanny said. Ant wished the night never had to end.

They rushed home, and Ant felt very tired. No wonder Nanny was always napping. Being a ninja was hard work. They climbed through the kitchen window and Nanny changed just in time as Mum came in from her night shift.

"You two look tired, you must have had fun last night," Mum said. Ant smiled secretly to himself. "Would you mind doing the same again tonight?" Mum asked Nanny.

"Yes!" said Ant. "Please can we, Nanny?"

"I'm sure we can find something to do," Nanny said. She winked at Ant, and Ant grinned from ear to ear. He thought Nanny might just be the most amazing person in the whole world.

The End

Book Bands for Guided Reading

Pink

Red

Yellow

Blue

Green

Orange

Turquoise

Purple

Gold

White

The Institute of Education book banding system is a scale of colours that reflects the various levels of reading difficulty. The bands are assigned by taking into account the content, the language style, the layout and phonics. Word, phrase and sentence level work is also taken into consideration.

Maverick Early Readers are a bright, attractive range of books covering the pink to white bands. All of these books have been book banded for guided reading to the industry standard and edited by a leading educational consultant.

Early Reader — Cool Duck and Lots of Hats

Early Reader — Catch It, Jess! and Cat Nap — by Katie Dale — Illustrated by Katia Dudina

Early Reader — The Space Race — by Jenny Jinks — Illustrated by Serena Lombardo

Early Reader — Pirates Don't Drive Diggers — by Alex English — Illustrated by Duncan Beedie

Early Reader — A Right Royal Mess

To view the whole Maverick Readers scheme, visit our website at www.maverickearlyreaders.com

Or scan the QR code above to view our scheme instantly!